Squirrel World

· A Park Pals Adventure ·

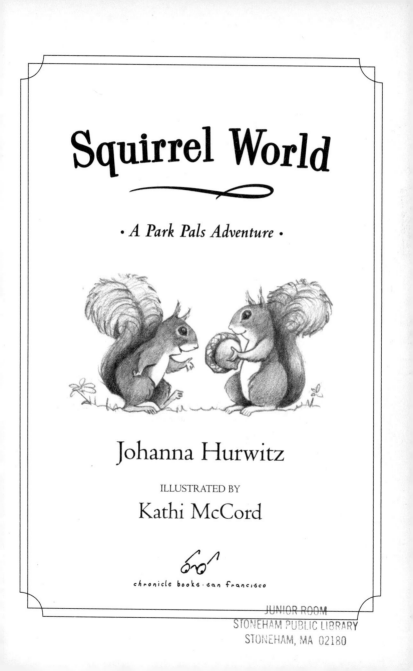

Johanna Hurwitz

ILLUSTRATED BY

Kathi McCord

chronicle books · san francisco

For Juliet, Fiona, & Ethan.
You're a special part of my world!
—J. H.

Text © 2007 by Johanna Hurwitz.
Illustrations © 2007 by Kathi McCord.

Typeset in Centaur and Pike.
The illustrations in this book were rendered in pencil.
Manufactured in China.

Library of Congress Cataloging-in-Publication Data
Hurwitz, Johanna.
Squirrel world / Johanna Hurwitz ; illustrated by Kathi McCord.
p. cm. — (Park pals adventure)
Summary: When Lexi the squirrel and his cousin Lenox leave Central Park to find the
New York City streets for which they were named, they discover that the human world
is wilder—and more dangerous—than they had ever imagined.
ISBN-13: 978-0-8118-5660-7
ISBN-10: 0-8118-5660-7
[1. Adventure and adventurers—Fiction. 2. Squirrels—Fiction. 3. City and town
life—Fiction. 4. New York (N.Y.)—Fiction. 5. Central Park (New York, N.Y.)
—Fiction.] I. Garry-McCord, Kathleen, ill. II. Title. III. Series.
PZ7.H9574Sq 2007
[Fic]—dc21
2006026714

Distributed in Canada by Raincoast Books
9050 Shaughnessy Street, Vancouver, British Columbia V6P 6E5

10 9 8 7 6 5 4 3 2 1

Chronicle Books LLC
680 Second Street, San Francisco, California 94107

www.chroniclekids.com

CONTENTS

NEW YORK CITY
East of Central Park

CHAPTER ONE

The Arrival of Spring

If you want to find me, look up. I'll be sitting on the highest branch of the tallest tree. I'm a squirrel, and I live in a park in the heart of New York City.

My name is Lexi, which is short for Lexington Avenue. It's a street that runs north and south in Manhattan. All the squirrels in the park are named for streets. There's Madison, Amsterdam, Columbus,

Lenox, Astor, Irving, and many others. In addition, because there are such a lot of us, many in my family have numerical names, just like the city streets. I have a fat, bossy uncle named Ninety-nine and sisters named Sixty-three and Sixty-four and Sixty-five.

Most squirrels spend their time running up and down tree trunks, jumping from branch to branch, chasing one another, and digging for and eating food. I do all those things, too. But last year I made a special friend who is not a squirrel. He's PeeWee, a guinea pig who was abandoned in the park. Without me, he wouldn't have survived a day, much less a whole year. I can't say I took him under my wing, because I don't have any wings. But I helped him find a place to live. I taught him what to eat and what to avoid. And I cheered him up when he felt homesick for his former home.

Nowadays PeeWee has a guinea pig mate, named Plush. They have four babies: Perky, Pudge, Pip, and Squeak. No one would believe that guinea pigs could survive the ice, snow, and cold of winter. My mother always told me, *"Don't be so sure of yourself that you fool yourself,"* and I tell you she was right. The guinea pigs managed to survive winter by moving into the rain forest at the park zoo. But now it is spring, and they are ready to return to their former home in the park.

On the day of their return, I was waiting up in a nearby tree. I watched and listened, and soon I heard PeeWee's voice.

"Good-bye, good-bye, good-bye," I heard him call to all his new rain-forest friends inside. *"Adiós, adiós, adiós,"* he added, using the Spanish word that he had learned from them.

Back in November, when the guinea pigs first arrived at the rain forest, it was easy to guess which were the parents and which were their children. Now, as they came into view, I saw that they were all comparable in size. In fact, Pudge was just a bit bigger than each of his parents. He loves to eat. Even Perky, who had once been very small and timid, had developed in the sunless damp of the rain

forest. And then there were Pip and Squeak. The two female guinea pigs are inseparable, spending all their time together, chattering to each other during the day and sleeping curled up against each other at night. Looking at the whole family, I knew they would no longer be able to live in one small hole.

"Come along," I heard Plush calling to her children.

"We know the way," Pudge responded. He hadn't gone two yards, and already he'd spotted something that looked edible.

"Watch your step," warned PeeWee. "Go at your own pace. We'll meet at our old tree this evening. Tomorrow evening at the latest, in case you get delayed. I'll have to start scouting out a couple of additional spaces. But remember, you're not safely inside the rain forest any longer. Watch out for dogs and bikes and baby carriages and humans and—"

"Oh, hush," Plush said to her mate. "One must be cautious in the park, but we can't be afraid to move about. People aren't expecting to see guinea pigs, so most of the time they won't see us. They'll think they're spotting dandelion fluff or a bird in the grass or some other thing. The last thing they're anticipating is a guinea pig."

"Hello there," I called down to my

friends. All the guinea pigs, even Pudge, looked around to see me.

"Hello, Lexi, what's up?" PeeWee shouted to me.

"The sky," I responded. "The sky is up."

"It's wonderful to see it," said PeeWee. "I missed it so while we were inside. And I missed you, too."

"Well, come along," I said to the guinea pigs. "I've already found a couple of possible homes for you, but you'd better hurry before some other animal moves inside."

"Oh, Lexi, you are so good to us," Plush called to me. "I've missed you during the winter." She paused a moment, taking a deep breath. "And I've missed the fresh air and the sun."

"And the seeds," said Pudge, his mouth full of food.

"You don't look as if you went hungry inside the rain forest," I commented.

"There was plenty for us to eat," PeeWee said. "And the other creatures were willing to share with us, too."

"But not much variety," grumbled Pudge, biting off a bud from a nearby bush.

"Look," called out Perky. "There's one of your cousins, Lexi."

"And there's another," called out Pip.

"And another," called out Squeak.

I didn't even turn my head to look. The park is filled with my cousins—and brothers and sisters, aunts and uncles. Sometimes we stop to greet one another or to chase one another up and down a tree, but mostly we're busy looking for our next meal. There's plenty to eat in the park, but until the food's inside our mouths, it doesn't count. *"Chew up your nut before you talk about it,"* my mother always used to say.

I watched as the guinea pigs began their journey home. Poor creatures. Their legs are so short that the guinea pigs move very slowly. A distance that I can cover in a moment with a single flying leap takes them many minutes to travel. And of course, guinea pigs don't have tails, and they can't climb trees. So although I'm very fond of them, I'm truly grateful that I was born a squirrel and not a guinea pig. A pair of humans walked by, and I thought to myself, thank goodness I'm not one of those creatures, either.

And then, because it was such a beautiful spring day and because I was feeling so especially pleased with life, I did one of my spectacular double somersaults from one tree branch to another.

CHAPTER TWO

Cousin Lenox

As I've mentioned, I have hundreds and hundreds of relatives all through the park. I've never bothered to make a full count of all of us, although once a human did attempt to do that. What humans don't know is that the best counters in the park are birds. They seem to be born with an ability to know numbers. It's a skill they need in order to keep track of the eggs in their nests.

The day that PeeWee and Plush left the rain forest, I arrived back at my tree home to discover an unexpected visitor. It was my cousin Lenox. I must confess he's not my favorite relative. He tends to be gloomy and grumpy much of the time. He complains a lot. It's as if every seed he ate were sour and every nut rotten. But as we had not seen each other in many, many months, I greeted him in the traditional friendly-squirrel manner: I chased him up and down my tree three times. We didn't attempt to speak. The chase is just a show of our speed and stamina and good health. Then, when we had completed this rite, Lenox joined me on a limb outside my nest.

"Well, Lenox," I said to him. "How has

the weather treated you? Did you enjoy the winter?"

"Winter, summer, spring, fall—it's all the same," grumbled Lenox.

"What do you mean?" I asked him. "Every day is different. Every day brings us something new: a nut, a seed, a flower, a friend."

Lenox scratched his right side with his left paw. Then he scratched his left side with his right paw. "I'm bored with nuts and seeds and flowers. And I haven't made a new friend in ages."

"Well, stick around for a few hours," I suggested. "My friends PeeWee and Plush and their children will be turning up later in the day. I think you'll enjoy them."

"PeeWee? Is that the fat furry fellow I've heard about? The one without a tail?"

"The very one," I said, nodding. "He doesn't have a tail, but he can read stories and poems to me," I bragged. PeeWee is the only nonhuman in the park who has mastered the art of reading. "He—"

"Forget him," said Lenox, interrupting. "I'm looking for something more exciting than a tailless creature. And I have a plan."

"What sort of a plan?" I asked, puzzled. It was not like Lenox to make plans.

"I want to take a journey, and I want a companion."

"Where do you want to go?" I asked my cousin.

"All my life I've been called Lenox. You've been called Lexington. Haven't you ever wanted to see the street that shares your name?"

"I don't know," I said. "Are there nuts there? Are there seeds?"

"Of course there are nuts and seeds on Lenox Avenue. It's covered with nuts. And so is Lexington Avenue," Lenox said confidently.

"How can you be so sure?" I asked him. "You've never been there."

"Why would our parents have named us for barren soil?" said Lenox. "I know these are fine places, and I want to go and see them. I want to go to Lenox Avenue. And I'm inviting you to join me."

"Thanks very much," I told him, "but no thanks. I'm staying right here."

"How can you give up this chance for an adventure?" Lenox demanded.

"It's easy," I said. "I'm satisfied with my life in the park."

"Please come," Lenox begged me.

I shook my head. I had no interest in Lenox Avenue at all.

"All right, then," he said. "I'll make a deal with you. We'll go to Lexington Avenue first. And after that, we'll go to Lenox Avenue."

"I'm still not interested," I said. "It's a long distance from here. It might take us a whole day. Maybe even two whole days."

"Of course. That's part of the adventure," my cousin said. "Think of all you'll see and taste along the way. Aren't you even a little bit tempted?"

I sat there thinking. In recent days, as spring arrived in the park, flocks of

migrating birds had returned, too. I had scanned the skies, watching for old friends. In some ways, I wasn't so different from the human bird-watchers who came to the park, carrying their peculiar devices for spying birds. I didn't need binoculars to see who had come home again. I also enjoyed sitting on a tree branch and eavesdropping on the conversations of the robins and some of the other birds. I heard them discuss their journeys to the south and back again. I'd never seen any part of the world except the park, and I admit that sometimes I envied the birds their opportunity to travel. I thought it must be wonderful to see other places, meet others of my species, sleep in new holes, and taste new foods.

I looked over at Lenox. It occurred to me that I'd never seen him show even a little bit of enthusiasm about anything. When the sun shines, he usually complains that we need rain. And of course when it rains, he grumbles that it's too wet. His usual attitude is not pleasant, and I guessed he'd been turned down by some of our other relatives before he arrived at my tree. I didn't believe I was his first choice for a traveling partner. And yet I began to realize that I was more than a little bit tempted by this idea of an adventurous journey to the street that bore my name.

I let Lenox nag a bit more while I thought about it. The average squirrel has a home range of about seven acres, but I have never been considered average. I've traveled all over the acreage of the park. Why shouldn't I travel still farther afield, like the birds? And so when Lenox finally stopped for breath and for new arguments, I found myself agreeing to accompany him. First we would go to Lexington Avenue, and afterward we'd travel to Lenox. He had won me over.

CHAPTER THREE

PeeWee Comes Home

"I've waited my whole life for this moment," Lenox declared triumphantly once I had agreed to accompany him. "Let's get going."

"If you've waited that long, it won't make much difference to wait another day," I told him.

This didn't please him at all.

"I want to be certain that PeeWee and Plush and their children arrive home safely.

And I want to show them the fine new tree holes I've found for them to live in, too."

"Since when have you gone into the real estate business?" asked Lenox, his voice full of disgust.

"Now listen here, Lenox," I said to him as patiently as I could. "If you want my company on this adventure of yours, then you'll have to agree to my terms. I'm not ready to depart today. So if you want to go now, go. Good-bye. Have a good time."

I had him there. Lenox talks big, but his courage is small. I knew he didn't want to go alone. And I also knew that there were not many other squirrels who would be willing to accompany Lenox when he ventured into the unknown. They did not want to risk falling off the edge of the world by going where they had never been before. Even my brother Columbus, named for an avenue that was named for a brave explorer, would not have wanted to leave his cozy nest on the west side of the park.

"What's safe is safe," my mother had taught us. But while Lenox might be motivated by boredom, I myself had a fascination with the unknown. The unknown is waiting to be known, I thought. I repeated that statement a couple of times to myself. I'd only just made it up, the way my mother had always made up her sayings. But the more I said it, the more I believed it. And the more I believed it, the more excited I felt about the adventure that Lenox and I were going to embark on. But I still felt a sense of responsibility to my guinea pig friends.

It was not until late afternoon that the exhausted band of guinea pigs arrived at their old home, just a few trees away from mine.

I introduced them to my cousin. "Lexi has more relatives than any other creature I've ever met," PeeWee said. "But the guinea pig clan is growing."

Even though she was very tired, Mother Plush immediately pushed her way inside their old tree hole. At once she began tossing out wet leaves that had blown inside during the winter.

She stuck her head outside. "It's too damp. This hole must dry out overnight before we can move back inside."

"And what about the size?" asked PeeWee. "Can we all fit in?"

He looked proudly at his grown offspring.

Plush shook her head. "Somehow our hole has become smaller while we were away."

"More likely, your family has grown bigger," I told her.

Then I led the way to the two new spots I'd located for them. Both were nearby and well hidden. It was quickly agreed that these new tree holes would perfectly serve the guinea pig family's needs. PeeWee was delighted that the holes were near each other. And all six guinea pigs were thrilled to discover the welcome-home banquet that I'd arranged for them: nuts, seeds, a cone from a human's ice cream, two apple cores, and half a doughnut. It had taken Lenox and me all afternoon to scout about and find these delicacies.

"How come you didn't have a feast waiting to welcome me?" Lenox had grumbled as he dug in the park soil.

"I wasn't expecting you," I reminded him.

Twice I'd caught him taking little bites from the food we'd collected.

"Lenox," I scolded him the second time. "If you aren't going to share and give, you aren't going to be a good traveling companion."

"No, no," he insisted. "I was just checking to be sure that nothing was rotten. You don't want to give your friends bad food."

I nodded and pretended to believe his excuse. But my words did serve to make him behave. Now PeeWee, Plush, and their four children began to eat. And as they were nibbling, gnawing, chewing, and chomping, I told them about the trip Lenox and I were planning to take.

Last spring, when he first arrived in the park, PeeWee would have been distraught by my news. He desperately needed me to watch

over him. But with time and my training, he has become totally familiar with the park world, and he now has a family of his own to watch over. I am happy to know we will be friends forever. However, now that he's got a mate, I know I'm not the number-one creature in his life. And it was just because I no longer had the enormous responsibility of protecting PeeWee that I could go off with Lenox.

"You will return here, won't you?" asked PeeWee.

"Of course," I reassured him. "My mother always said, *'East, west, one's nest is best.'*"

"You will have many good stories to tell us when you come home," commented Plush, looking up from the apple core she was holding in her paws.

"You may find another world that you like better," PeeWee pointed out.

"Impossible," I insisted.

I reminded myself that unlike all the other rodents in the park, PeeWee had not been born here. He was born in a pet shop and had for a brief time been the pet of a young human. So he'd already seen other worlds. In fact, it had taken him time to adjust to this life, with its freedom and its dangers.

I didn't know much about Lexington Avenue, but I knew that even if I liked it better than the park, I'd come back. I'd tell my stories to PeeWee and Plush and their children. And I had promised Lenox that we'd go in search of Lenox Avenue, too. I had a lot of adventures ahead of me.

I turned to Lenox, who had joined the guinea pigs at their meal and was busily chewing on one of the seeds we'd gathered.

"We leave at dawn," I announced to him and to the others.

Lenox swallowed the seed and let out a cheer. "It's about time," he grumbled, as if I'd been keeping him waiting for weeks.

CHAPTER FOUR

I Leave Home

Now here's the truth of the matter: There had to be a reason why I'd never gone off to see this Lexington Avenue place before. After all, you'd think I'd have been curious. And the fact is, I was. But I was not so curious that I'd have deserted my wonderful home and my enormous family and set off on my own. So when Lenox suggested we go together, I realized that this was my chance.

But there was another part to the truth: I was scared.

In the park, there are thousands of trees that I can climb for safety. There are bushes to hide behind, holes to slip into, and enough brothers, sisters, aunts, uncles, and cousins to confuse anyone trying to find me. Out on the city streets, who knew where a squirrel could find safety? Still, I was determined to go through with the plan.

I crawled into my hole for the night and curled up, making room for my visitor. After complaining briefly that he felt cramped, Lenox fell fast asleep. I remained awake. I lay quietly and savored the familiar smell of my nest. I stuck out a paw and touched each of my treasures that was close by. They were all things that I had found in the park.

I had two unmatched mittens lost by small humans. I had several metal disks called coins that humans exchange for ice cream, bags of peanuts, or balloons in warm weather, when the vendors come into the park.

My newest and most favorite possession was a woolen cap with a funny top called a pom-pom that I'd watched a man remove from his head on an unseasonably warm day. He had stuffed this human head covering into his pocket, but from my perch on a tree branch I had noticed that the cap was sticking halfway in and halfway out. I had a feeling that it might come all the way out if I waited patiently. Sure enough, as the man walked, the cap worked its way free of the pocket. It landed softly on the ground, and instantly I pounced on it, picked it up in my teeth, and climbed with it up the nearest tree. The man never noticed at all.

However, old Uncle Ninety-nine happened to observe me. "That's not edible, you know," he called out.

But unlike my uncle, I think of more than just my stomach. I knew that the cap would make a warm, cozy lining for my nest. I removed the cap from my mouth just long enough to call out to him, "A nut this large would make me sick." Then, securing the cap firmly between my teeth, I ran and leaped and made it all the way home.

Now I snuggled deep inside the cap. The evening was cool, and I was glad to have the cap. I wished there were a way that I could bring this wonderful possession along with me on my travels, but I knew that was

impossible. It will be waiting here for me when I return, I thought.

The next thing I knew, the first faint light of morning was showing, and Lenox was poking me.

"Come on, come on," he chattered impatiently. When he saw me stirring, he climbed outside.

I stretched and scratched my head and then jumped out to the limb where Lenox was standing. "Hold your fleas," I told him. "I'm ready to go."

It was quiet in the park so early in the morning. No humans were in sight. Only a few birds were softly beginning their daily songs. I saw a robin pulling a large worm from the ground. I knew he was going to bring it to his mate, who was already sitting on a nest of blue eggs.

By the time Lenox and I passed this way again, the eggs would probably have hatched.

"This is a good place, isn't it?" I said to Lenox as we raced toward the eastern edge of the park.

"Now don't change your mind. Don't back out of our plan," said Lenox, looking at me nervously.

"I don't break my promises," I told him. "But I can still admire this place. After all, spring is the best time here, with all the new buds and seedpods and more people coming and dropping their food on the ground." I paused and thought a moment. "Well, summer is pretty special too: all the trees lush and green, hordes of people having picnics, and the trash bins overflowing. Then there's autumn—"

"Stop, stop!" shouted Lenox. "One more minute and you are going to talk yourself out of this trip."

So I closed my mouth, and as we ran I remembered jumping into mounds of leaves in the autumn. It's the most fun imaginable. Well, except for playing in the winter. I love to make tracks on freshly fallen snow. My squirrel world in the park is absolutely the most wonderful life one could ever ask for.

It didn't take long for us to reach the eastern edge of the park. There's a wide avenue there called Fifth. One of my sisters is named Fifth, too. During the day there are a lot of humans walking both ways along the avenue. There's also loads of traffic on wheels—cars, buses, trucks, and bicycles. For some reason, the traffic goes in only one direction: south. But it was still so early in the morning that the avenue was quiet. Lenox and I could cross the broad street with ease. As I turned my head to look back at the park, I hoped the streets that lay ahead of us would be as simple to cross.

"Look how dull it is here without trees," I commented to Lenox as we continued on our way. There were tall buildings on both sides of the street but only an occasional square of earth with a tree managing to grow out of it. Beneath our feet was hard cement. In one or two places, where there was a crack, tiny blades of grass were trying hard to grow.

"There's more to life than trees," said Lenox. "I'm sure when we reach Lexington Avenue, we'll find all sorts of other things to delight us."

"I don't know where you get that idea," I told him. But I kept going on. By the time we reached the next avenue, which is named Madison, my paws were aching. Lenox must have felt the same way, for he grumbled, "I don't like walking on cement."

"Humans don't seem to mind," I responded. "Perhaps it's because they wear coverings on their feet—shoes, boots, sandals."

"Paws are best," said Lenox. "And when we reach Lexington Avenue, the ground will be soft and comforting."

I could see that he was limping from pain. Luckily, one of the few trees was at hand. "Let's climb up here and take a rest," I suggested.

"If you insist," said Lenox, running quickly up the tree, which was a ginkgo. I joined him, and the two of us licked our swollen paws to comfort them. Of course, there are cement walks throughout the park, but no squirrel remains very long on the hard, rough ground when there is soft, cool earth nearby.

As we sat on an upper branch of the tree, we observed the nature of the day constantly changing. First a few and then more and more people and cars passed by us. Just like in the park, there were equal numbers of people going in either direction, all of them very focused on wherever they were headed. They didn't take any time to stop and look around. Humans are very strange.

Fortunately, humans are also hungry. It wasn't long before there were dropped bits of bagels and doughnuts in the trash can near the base of the tree. I jumped down and foraged for a good snack. Some pigeons flew overhead, waiting till we'd dropped some crumbs on the ground for them. So I obliged and broke off a bit of doughnut. Instantly a dozen more pigeons appeared out of nowhere.

"Don't," cautioned Lenox. "We don't want to make a spectacle of ourselves."

But no one stopped to watch. Pigeons and squirrels seemed invisible to the humans on the street.

After eating, Lenox and I decided it was time to digest our meal. So we each picked a crook of the tree and took a snooze. So far, our adventure had been pretty tame, and I was thankful for that. I didn't know that things were going to change very shortly.

CHAPTER FIVE

A Hole in the Ground

After a short rest, I decided we should continue. "Are you ready to go on?" I asked Lenox.

He opened his eyes, scratched himself, and nodded. "Of course," he said. "I was waiting for you."

We jumped down and continued east. The day was changing. Instead of warming up, as days usually do, a brisk wind was blowing. The sky had started to grow darker, and it became evident that it was going to rain before long. Squirrels never mind rain. The water disposes of fleas and fills puddles for us to drink from. And when we've had enough rain, we give ourselves a good shake to dry our fur and then cuddle up in a tree hole. But here, outside the park, the trees were too small and young to have deep, protective holes. I didn't look forward to rain the way I would have inside the park.

Sure enough, before we had gone very far, the rain began to fall. All around us, humans opened their rain protectors, held them over their heads, and walked faster than ever. Lenox and I had to watch out for their feet. Twice I just missed being kicked by a hurrying human.

"The rain is wetter here than in the park," Lenox complained to me.

"Rain is rain," I replied. "It's all the same everywhere."

"No, no," he insisted. "It will be better on Lexington Avenue. It will be less wet and less cold there."

I didn't see how Lexington Avenue could possibly live up to my cousin's expectations.

We reached the next street, which I knew was Park Avenue. I had always assumed that the name meant it was really another park. My bird friends who have flown all over the city have told me that there are more than 1,700 parks in New York, which cover more than 28,000 acres. Well, if this counted as one of those parks, what a joke! There was a bit of grass in the middle of the street, but no trees, no benches, no bushes—nothing. What a ridiculous park this is, I thought as the rain continued to drip off my fur. Nevertheless, I automatically found myself sniffing and digging a hole. There could be a nut buried in the soil, I thought. I found nothing. After a second unsuccessful try, I realized it was useless. There were no other squirrels around to have buried anything for us to find.

"Come on, come on," nagged Lenox.

And so we went on again, crossing onto the cement.

Just when we were both as wet as we'd ever been in our lives, we noticed great numbers of humans heading toward a gigantic hole in the ground.

We both paused for a moment and then did what any wet animal would do: We went into the hole, too. There was a steep flight of steps to help the humans make their way down. Luckily, there are steps in some areas of the park, so both Lenox and I knew how to use them.

Midway down, I heard the most horrible roar. The ground vibrated, and I put my paws over my ears to shut out the intense noise and ran to a corner of the stairwell. Some birds who had returned from a winter in South America once told me about an earthquake. I was sure an earthquake had come to New York now. But just as I was about to resign myself to a certain end, the roar stopped with a terrible screeching sound. Then it was quiet.

"What was that?" asked Lenox, shaking with fright.

"I think it was an earthquake," I told him. "But look how brave the humans are. They don't seem to be afraid of it at all."

We watched as the figures on the steps kept moving. Many went downward. But now there was an equal number moving upward. Can't they make up their minds? I wondered.

I was just about to move downward again too when the sound returned. Lenox and I cowered with fear on the steps for many minutes. Eventually I began to see a pattern: the loud sounds, the screeching, the quieter times, and then the loud sounds again—and through it all, humans walking in both directions.

"Those noises don't mean a thing," said Lenox. "Look how the people keep moving toward them."

"Yes. But see how there are other people going in the other direction," I pointed out.

"But they don't look as if they've been injured in any way. It's obviously perfectly safe. The noise must just be meant to keep bad creatures away."

There seemed to be some logic to Lenox's statement. So I bravely followed him, and we continued to the end of the flight of stairs. The area was dark as night but lit by small man-made moons. We looked around us and saw a large dark tunnel. There are tunnels in the park, too. I wondered where this one led and whether we should run into it.

"Look, there are squirrels down here!" called out a human voice.

"They must be lost," someone said.

"We're not lost at all," chattered Lenox indignantly. "We know exactly where we're going."

But of course humans can't understand us the way we can understand them.

Suddenly the vibrations and racket began again. We watched in horror as first lights and then a huge silver object came out of a tunnel toward us. I shuddered to think

what would have become of us had we been
inside the tunnel.

Because we were closer than ever, the sound
was louder than ever. But again it screeched
to a halt. Doors on the silver object opened,
and people got out. Others went in. I guessed
it was a type of very noisy bus.

"Are the squirrels going to take the
subway?" a human called out as he entered
the vehicle.

The people standing around began to laugh.

"Did they pay for a ride?" someone called out.

The doors closed while Lenox and I watched, mesmerized.

Then the huge object began moving, accompanied by the horrific noise, with that poor, helpless person inside.

"Humans are insane," I told Lenox. "Why would they voluntarily enter such an object when they can be above ground, where it is quieter and prettier?"

"And wetter," he reminded me.

"I'd much rather be wet than have my eardrums assaulted," I said.

"Are you afraid?" asked Lenox.

"No," I said. I thought a moment. What was wrong with admitting fear? "Well, maybe I am. But whatever—there must be a better way to keep dry. And a better way to get to Lexington Avenue."

I turned in the direction from which we had come and ran back up the stairway.

"Don't leave me!" shrieked Lenox. And he followed after me. He might not have wanted to admit it, but he was afraid, too.

CHAPTER SIX

Lexington Avenue

You might be wondering how Lenox and I would know Lexington Avenue when we reached it. The answer is simple: When I was an infant, my mother sang me to sleep with a special squirrel lullaby. The song included all the street names on the east side of the park, in order from east to west.

It went like this:

> *Close your eyes and count the streets,*
> *soon you will be fast asleep.*
> *East End Avenue, then comes York,*
> *on to First, Second, Third,*
> *flying high just like a bird.*
> *Lexington, Park, Madison, and Fifth,*
> *life is great, it is a gift.*
> *Singing sweetly as a lark,*
> *home is best in Central Park.*

I'd heard those words a thousand times, so of course I knew the names of all the avenues to the east of the park. Similarly, Lenox's mother had sung a variation of that song to him, using the streets surrounding his namesake avenue. Now headed toward

Lexington Avenue, I reversed the order of the streets in the lullaby. We'd passed Fifth, Madison, and Park. When we came up to street level again, I knew we were close to Lexington Avenue. We moved closer, and I stared at it with great disappointment. It appeared to be about as ugly a place as one could imagine. Why had my mother thought to give me its name?

Lenox must have had the same idea. "This is not a very special place at all," he complained. "Wait until we get to Lenox Avenue. I know that is much better."

"You don't know that at all," I retorted. "Both the streets we were named after are mysteries. It's quite possible that our parents had never seen either one. Maybe they just liked the way the names sounded."

"I don't believe it," declared my cousin. "Lenox Avenue is a beautiful place."

As we talked, we moved toward one of the puny trees that was growing out of a square of dirt. If nothing else, the little tree offered us a branch above the crowd. It was no longer raining, but the day remained overcast. It was quite likely we'd see more rain before long.

We sat there on the same branch, glaring at each other. I was annoyed that I'd wasted a day getting to this place. It was better to dream about Lexington Avenue than to actually see it.

Lenox grumbled, "We should have gone directly to Lenox Avenue."

"Don't tell me what we should have done," I retorted. "This was all your plan. I was happy at home."

A couple of humans standing close to the tree were having a discussion, too. "I'm not going into another museum for a month," the man declared. "Maybe not for a year," he added after a moment.

"It's all right. We've seen the three big ones now. And we'll tell everyone that we went to the others. Who will know? It's hard work being a tourist," the woman admitted.

"Let's go back to our hotel. I want to take my shoes off," the man said.

"See?" I said to Lenox. "Even human feet get tired walking on cement."

Before my cousin could respond, the woman let out a loud wail of protest. "Oh, no!" she cried. "We're right here on Lexington Avenue, which is where Bloomingdale's is located. We must go there. I can't go home to Springfield without first seeing Bloomingdale's. You know how much I've wanted to go there."

"All right, all right," the man agreed reluctantly. Suddenly the woman grabbed his arm. "Look!" she shouted. "Here's a bus coming. We can jump on, and we'll get there right away. I promise. After that, we'll go back to the hotel."

We watched as the couple raced to catch the huge bus. The doors opened, and some people got out. The man and woman waited to get on.

"Come," I called to Lenox and leaped down off my perch on the tree. "Didn't you hear what that woman said? We must go to Blooming Dales, too. That must be why Lexington Avenue is famous."

"And how are we going to find this

Blooming Dales place?" Lenox shouted after me.

"Just like the humans. We'll take the bus."

With that I leaped onto a metal piece on the rear of the vehicle. Not a moment too soon, Lenox joined me.

"This had better be good," he said.

"It will. It will. Just hold on tight. We'll get off when that man and woman do. That's how we'll know where we're going."

The bus lurched and started moving.

"Hold tight!" I shouted.

Lenox held on tight, and so did I.

CHAPTER SEVEN

In Search of Blooming Vales

Our ride was a bumpy one. One moment we thought we were about to be thrown off, and the next thing we knew the bus was slowing to a stop. But just as we were about to relax our hold, it took off again. It's not easy riding on a bus, I decided. No wonder I'd never tried it before.

At one of our stops, Lenox asked me, "What does it mean—Blooming Dales?"

I wasn't certain, but I wasn't going to tell him that. "Let's figure it out," I said as the bus began to move again. "The first part is easy: I've heard people in the park talk about the plants. They look at the flowers and say, 'What lovely blooms.' Or they say, 'The flowers are blooming.' Obviously *blooming* means 'flowering.'"

"And *dales*?" Lenox asked.

I paused a moment, thinking hard. *Dales? Dales?* I knew I'd heard the word before.

Suddenly it came to me. I'd heard the word in one of the poems that PeeWee read aloud. How did it go?

> *I wandered lonely as a cloud*
> *that floats on high o'er vales and hills . . .*

Oh, dear. I was wrong. The poem said *vales* and not *dales.* The tourist had probably gotten it confused. She meant to say *vales*, I decided. And I'd learned from PeeWee that *vales* means "valleys."

"Flowering valleys!" I shouted to Lenox, as the bus took off again. I was delighted that my reasoning had produced such a happy answer to our question. "Lexington Avenue may be a disappointment," I told my cousin, "but Blooming Vales, which is another part of the avenue, will be magnificent." I began to imagine an area filled with golden daffodils, brilliant red tulips, white and purple lilac bushes, bright pink rhododendron plants, and lush soft green grass. No matter that in our park each of those flowers blooms in a different week. In Blooming Vales, those and a hundred different varieties would all be in flower at the same time. Also, unlike this part of Lexington Avenue, there would be no more cement and no rain.

"We'll be there soon," I promised Lenox. I could hardly wait.

Each time the bus stopped, its doors opened. Some people got on, and some people got off. Lenox and I watched carefully. Humans look more or less the same to us, so we had to be sure that we didn't confuse the couple we were following with another pair, a couple who was going somewhere else.

"That's them!" I shouted to Lenox as the bus came to another stop and I saw the man and woman we were following get off.

We jumped down from our perch. I was relieved to be on firm ground again, even if it was cement. We watched as the couple stood looking about. Then they began to cross to the other side of the street.

"Come along!" I shouted to Lenox.

I was so busy watching the couple that I didn't have time to look around. But from the corner of my eye, I could see that this part of Lexington Avenue looked no more interesting than the part where we'd been before.

"They're going inside that building," said Lenox.

"Then we have to follow them," I replied. "It must lead to Blooming Vales."

We stood waiting for someone to pull open one of the big doors, and then we scooted quickly inside.

At once, I could sense that I was in a place that was unlike any I'd ever been in before.

I could smell the perfume of flowers. It was much stronger and sweeter than the perfume of the flowers in the park. But when I looked around, I couldn't see any flowers at all. There were paths leading in all directions, and Lenox and I didn't know which way to run first.

"Look! I never saw a squirrel inside the store before!" shouted someone.

"There are two of them!"

"Make yourself scarce!" I called out to Lenox. I was afraid someone would attempt to chase us away before we'd had the chance

to explore all that this strange building had to offer.

The floor was shiny and slippery, not like cement and not like soil. I could hear my paws scratching as I ran. Luckily, there were so many people and so many nooks and crannies that even without trees or shrubs to hide in, Lenox and I quickly managed find a dark corner in which to keep safe.

We stayed hidden for quite a while. It was good to sit quietly and catch our breath. Since early morning, we had been running on hard cement, exposed to outrageous noises, and bumped about on the back of a bus. Now we both curled up, watching and listening but not making a movement that might call attention to us. My stomach reminded me that I hadn't eaten in hours, and I wondered where the food was stored in this place.

"We've got to get out of here," Lenox said firmly. "I don't care what the name means. There are no flowering valleys here."

I hated to admit it, but he was right.

Maybe there was something better on the other side of the street, I thought.

Cautiously, keeping low and frequently hiding, Lenox and I headed back in the direction we had come from. It was a great relief when I saw the doors again, and when someone opened one, I charged out. Lenox was right behind me. We'd escaped from Blooming Vales. Now what?

I looked around. The street was crowded with people walking in both directions. There were cars and buses, noise and feet. This was not a good place for a pair of squirrels.

Then I looked across the street. I saw a large building with a huge sign on it. I tried to remember the reading lessons PeeWee had given me last summer.

I had already mastered all 26 letters of the alphabet. So I quickly recognized *N* and *U*. N-U. I tried to sound out the letters as PeeWee had been trying to teach me to do. N-U-T. Was that Noot? No, no, I realized with delight.

"Nut! It says nut!" I shouted happily to Lenox.

That's where I made a very big mistake. I didn't pay any attention to the other letters:

R-U-S . . . What did they matter? Nothing is more important when you're hungry than an N-U-T.

"Come quickly!" I cried. "That's where we have to go."

Once again we ran with every bit of speed we could muster. And once again we jumped through an open door. And alas. Once again we were in a flowery, scented house with no flowers, no trees, and no nuts. How could that sign have lied? I was furious.

"Squirrels! Look at the squirrels!" someone shouted.

The people standing nearby began to squeal and jump about. You'd think they'd never seen a squirrel before in their lives.

"I'm starving," said Lenox, ignoring the humans. "I must find something to eat."

For once the two of us were in agreement. We ran about sniffing the air. There had to be food somewhere. How could this store have such a big sign for nuts and yet not have a single nut in sight?

Suddenly a huge cloth was thrown over us, and Lenox and I were trapped underneath it. We fought to get out, but the cloth was too heavy for us. We could hardly move.

"I'm going to suffocate," yelled Lenox, trying to push the cloth away.

"Wait. Wait. Let me think," I said, attempting to remain calm. I knew we shouldn't try to fight off the covering. We needed to save our energy. Someone would have to remove it. The humans wanted to get rid of us as much as we wanted to be rid of them.

CHAPTER EIGHT

Trapped

Since we couldn't escape, we did the only sensible thing we could, which was to curl up and go to sleep. With a good rest behind us, we'd both be able to think better.

We woke to the sound of human voices and to the sensation of human hands in thick gloves lifting us up and putting us into a closed box with mesh sides. I ran around in a panic.

I could look out of the box, but there was no way to get out.

"Stop! I smell something good!" shouted Lenox with excitement.

I stopped and took a deep breath. "I do too," I said.

We ran toward the scent, which was like peanuts but even stronger and better. "It's like smashed peanuts," Lenox said, eating something he found in the corner of the box. "And it's delicious. I love it."

He was right. It was delicious. But though I was very hungry, I still was sharp enough to realize we were in a terrible situation. "Don't you see what has happened?" I cried out in despair.

Lenox looked up, his mouth covered with the tan peanut paste. He licked it from his

lips. He looked around for the first time. "We're in a cage!" he cried out. "Look what you did. You got us trapped inside a cage."

Lenox and I ran round and round the mesh cage that we found ourselves in. Never mind that at one end the delicious peanut smell was wafting over us. A cage is the worst possible place that a squirrel can be. There had to be a way for us to get out.

And if there wasn't a way out, what did the humans plan to do with us?

Eventually we were both exhausted. We had to stop, and while we caught our breath, I finally could overhear talk of the proposed scheme for Lenox and me.

"They belong in a park," a man's voice said with certainty.

"Yes, but I've come up with a better idea. In fact, it's an extraordinary one," said another voice.

"What's that?"

"You know the display that our window decorators have just set up? It's a park scene with mannequins, plants, and fake birds. Imagine if we had *real* squirrels running up and down the plants. People would flock to see our windows. It would be fantastic.

Better than Bloomingdale's. Better than Lord and Taylor. Better than Macy's. Our window would be better than any of those windows with mechanical objects. This would be *real*. We can call it Squirrel World."

"Do you really think people will stop and look at our windows?" another man asked.

"Of course. Haven't you ever walked past that pet shop on Sixtieth Street? There's always a crowd admiring the dogs in the window. Imagine the people looking at our squirrels. It would be fantastic. And after they finished looking at the windows, they'd come inside and shop. That's what it's all about: attracting customers to buy our Nu-Tru Styles."

Nu-Tru Styles. I shuddered when I heard those words. I'd once overheard one human

tell another that a little learning is a dangerous thing. My little bit of learning had misled
me to believe that this was a store that sold
nuts. How could I have been so dumb?

The two men continued their talking. I
grew tired trying to follow all they had to
say. Finally, despite my fears, my hunger
got the better of me, and I began nibbling
again at the peanut paste. It was sticky stuff,
almost as if someone had pre-chewed it for
us. It was good, but nothing could be good
enough to make up for being in a cage.

Eventually Lenox and I were let out of the
cage. For one glorious moment, I thought we
were free. But then I realized we had traded
one cage for another. In place of the small
mesh cage, we were now in a much larger
space, which looked out onto Lexington

Avenue. I made a flying leap and hit my head on an invisible barrier. It was clear glass, the same stuff that they use for car and bus windows. Stunned, I lay on the ground. It seemed to be earth, but actually it was some sort of imitation, made out of paper.

I looked around me. It appeared that we were inside the park. There was a bench with a pair of humans sitting on it. One was holding a newspaper and reading. Nearby

were two children who appeared to be playing. One had a ball, and the other had a pail
and shovel. I watched them. No one moved.
Not a breath, not a blink. I stared at the large
humans. The man never turned a page in his
paper, and the woman never glanced at the
children. Time passed, and the children never
dug in the dirt or whined for ice cream.

I climbed up a tree, but it wasn't a true
tree, made of wood and bark. I chewed on a
leaf, and it tasted like paper. In fact, it *was*
paper. I jumped over to another tree. Perhaps
that one would be better. It wasn't. Nothing
smelled or tasted or felt as it should inside
this huge cage.

"Oh, Lenox," I sighed aloud. "What have
we gotten ourselves into? There is nothing
real in this place but us."

CHAPTER NINE

"Squirrel World"

What followed were days of captivity inside the fake world. I suppose to some it might have seemed glorious. Without the slightest effort on our part, our hunger and thirst were satisfied. Ample amounts of food and water were provided. Each morning, fresh supplies of peanuts were thrown at us. There were enough to keep us well fed all day long.

But gradually we grew bored with the sameness of our diet.

I also suddenly understood what my mother had meant when she said, *"If you don't put in a day's work, you will not find fun in your day."* Though we had nothing to do but eat and chase each other, I grew more and more restless. There was not much satisfaction or triumph in finding food when I didn't have to look for it. Furthermore, large as this new cage was, it could not compare with our home in the park. Lenox and I ran up and down the phony trees, chasing each other, but we had no other squirrels to play with.

There was constant sunshine, always coming from the same angle, until it suddenly went out at night. I had never realized how much I loved the variety of weather.

Here it never rained. There were no breezes. Even worse, there were no birds or insects or any other life at all. Just Lenox and me running around and getting more and more bored with each other and our limited existence.

It reminded me of something, and I confess I was slow to realize what it was. "We are just like creatures in the park zoo," I gasped when it finally dawned on me. "This is what it must be like for them."

"Yes. And *you* got us into this situation," Lenox berated me over and over again, once he tired of our life in the store window.

It was no use reminding him that this expedition to Lexington Avenue had been his idea. Who knew that Blooming Vales had only fake flowers in bloom? Who knew that Nu-Tru Styles was a prison? Who knew that we would end up trapped in a cage with humans? Humans who weren't even real!

When we became too bored to run around, we looked out at the people who were looking at us. Men, women, and children stood in rapt amazement, watching us. Yes, indeed, it was exactly like being an animal in the zoo.

In fact, I don't remember ever seeing such mobs around a single zoo cage. Big and small humans pressed their noses to the window. After a while, we noticed that there were many humans marching back and forth, holding big sticks attached to cardboard signs with messages written on them. I could read some of the letters: A-S-P-C-A. I had no idea what those letters spelled. I certainly needed more lessons from PeeWee.

But I feared I'd never see him or my squirrel family in the park ever again.

Sometimes police officers in their blue uniforms would argue with the people. We couldn't hear what they said, but we obviously were the focus of everyone's attention.

I tapped on the glass window, and I could see that the people were delighted. Immediately someone tapped back.

"Fools!" I called to the humans. "If you want to see trees and squirrels, go to the park."

But they paid no attention. During the course of the day, more and more people stood spellbound. Sometimes bright lights flashed at us as people with cameras took our picture. I thought of the millions of times I had watched humans taking pictures of one another in the park. Some of the cameras spit out the picture at once, so over the years I have seen some of the results. Often people leave the pictures on park benches or in the trash cans. Blurred copies of nature, totally inedible. They serve no purpose at all.

When the sun went off at nighttime, Lenox and I stopped performing. We sat under the phony trees and discussed our situation. "If only we could find a way out," he said to me.

But we had searched every corner of our cage, and there seemed to be no crack or hole. There was a sliding door that opened briefly every morning, when the day's supply of food and water was left for us. But it all happened so quickly that there was no way for us to make a break for it. And if we did, then what? We would end up back inside the store. We'd once again be running away from all those people who had chased us before.

Occasionally a pigeon or two walked past the window. I tried to attract their attention. Maybe they would fly to the park and get some of our family to help us. But even when I tapped at the pigeons, they just looked up and then away. They seemed to care only about food. They didn't care about trapped squirrels.

"I hate it here," said Lenox. Had he told me that a hundred times? Or was it two hundred?

I totally agreed with him, but I didn't tell him that. What was the point of it? I tried to think of the good things about our situation. We were safe. Dogs passed by all day long. Some of them pulled at their leashes and tried to get through the window, but they couldn't. They growled and pressed their muzzles against the glass, but they couldn't reach us. In the park, we often had to run from dogs that got free from their owners. I know of more than one squirrel who found himself or herself between the jaws of an unleashed dog.

There was another good thing about our situation: We had food. There was no doubt where our next meal was coming from. There was also no doubt what our next meal would be. That made it boring, of course. There's excitement and surprise when you go off looking for food. True, on some days we find more and better meals than on others. But now I yearned for a day of digging and scratching and hunting for food. An empty stomach back home was better than a meal in this prison.

CHAPTER TEN

I Make a Plan

"I hate this. I hate this!" Lenox screamed at me as he ran in circles around our limited space every evening when the sun was turned off and all the people were gone.

"Hating doesn't change things," I said finally, trying not to shout back at him. Lenox's constant complaining did not make things any easier for me. I tried to think of one of my mother's phrases. In the past, they had always kept me going. I began reciting them quietly to myself. My wise mother had taught me so much: *"A nut in the jaw is worth two in the paw."* *"Look before you eat."* *"A leap in time is mighty fine."* *"Don't count your nuts before they are shelled."* *"Don't cry over a rotten nut."*

"Stop that mumbling. You're driving me nuts!" shrieked Lenox.

"Driving me nuts." I've heard humans use that expression, and it never makes sense. It makes even less sense when a squirrel says it, although I confess that Lenox's constant whining and yelling did make me want to take a bite out of him.

"I'm trying to think of what my mother would have done," I told Lenox. "There has to be a way out of this situation. If she were here, she'd have figured it out already."

"But she's not!" Lenox shouted. "You'd better hurry and do something!"

"Hold your fleas," I told him. I had just remembered one of my mother's sayings: *"Any squirrel who climbs up a tree can climb down a tree, too."*

"Now just what is that supposed to mean?" grumbled Lenox when I repeated it for him. "We don't even have a decent tree in this place. Just these phony paper imitations."

"When my mother said, 'Any squirrel who climbs up a tree can climb down a tree, too,' it was back in the days when my siblings and I were learning how to go up and down tree trunks. Going up always seemed easier to us. When we were climbing down, we were all terrified of looking where we were going.

We were certain we would fall."

"We can't fall here. We can hardly *climb* here," said Lenox.

"Well, of course, I know that," I replied. "But what she really meant was that if you get into a situation, you can get out of it."

"That's no help to us whatsoever!" shouted Lenox.

Well, it was no help to *him.* But I'd lived with my mother long enough to have learned that every saying has a second meaning behind it. Her words encouraged me to keep thinking. If we had gotten into this big glass-enclosed cage, we could get out of it. And an hour later, I came up with a plan.

"Listen," I said to Lenox. "Why are we in here?" And then before he could say that it was because of me or because I was named for Lexington Avenue or any other reason that he could blame on me, I continued. "We're in this window as a display. People are coming to look at us. It brings attention to the store. But suppose instead of running up and down these phony trees, we acted as if we were fake, too? That would certainly bore everyone, and the people would go away. Then the store owners wouldn't want us in the window any longer."

"What do you mean, 'act as if we're fake'?" asked Lenox. "We're real. We can't be fake."

"Of course we're real. But you know in the park how they have all those statues? There's the girl sitting with a book on her lap and the man with children around him. There's a dog and a man riding a horse.

They're made of metal, and they look real, but they're not. They don't move. We can pretend that we're made of metal and keep still. If we don't do anything, there will be no point in watching us."

"It sounds easy enough," Lenox admitted reluctantly. He was so used to complaining to me that he hated to give me credit for coming up with a good idea.

"All right," I said. "That's what we'll do. Tomorrow morning when the people start coming and staring at us, we'll hold perfectly still. Even when you breathe, try to be unnoticeable."

"What about eating?" asked Lenox.

"No eating. Eat right now if you want to. But no eating while there are people around."

Lenox immediately ran to search for one of the nuts that our captors threw into the window each day. He ate two nuts before he settled down for the night.

I ate one nut myself before going to sleep. I could hardly wait for the morning to come so we could set our plan into motion, or nonmotion, as the case was.

As soon as we woke, I reminded Lenox: "No moving." Then I posed myself in front of the fake tree. Lenox went and sat near the park bench.

"This should be easy," he said.

It was not easy. Have you ever tried to stand perfectly still hour after hour? People walked by the window as usual. They looked at us, and I noticed they were talking more than ever. I blinked my eye, and I heard a shout from someone. I knew I had to be more careful.

More people came, and they all stared hard. It had become a challenge for them to see if we moved. I hoped they thought we were stuffed toys. I've seen many in the park being dragged about by little children—furry little animal toys with no power to move. I really hoped we would seem just like one of them.

"This is so boring," said Lenox, dropping his pose and scratching himself. Immediately there were such loud cheers from the people outside that we could hear them inside our glass prison.

"Stop scratching!" I shouted, turning to Lenox.

"You're moving!" he yelled back.

The people outside continued to cheer. I turned to face them and saw that for all my planning, we had managed to attract more people than ever before. My plan was an absolute failure.

CHAPTER ELEVEN
Another Plan

"Any squirrel who climbs up a tree can climb down a tree," my mother had said. Back in my childhood, when I couldn't grasp a tree trunk from one angle, I learned to change course quickly and shoot my paw out toward another piece of tree bark. If my plan didn't work, then there was only one thing to do: devise another plan.

And after much thought, another idea

came to me. "Suppose instead of attracting good attention, we embarrassed the store owners?" I said to Lenox. "Suppose they didn't want people to see us? If we did something bad, they'd want to get us out of the window at once."

"So how do you plan to do that?" asked Lenox grumpily. He was angrier than ever since my first plan had failed. "We're helpless. We can't do anything while we're trapped in here," he said.

"Yes, we can. I've figured it all out," I said.

"Just like you figured it all out before," Lenox sneered.

"Stop being so negative, and listen to me," I scolded him. "If we chew up these phony trees and destroy this make-believe world, it won't look very eye-catching at all."

Lenox stood in front of me and scratched his back. "Do you think that will really work?" he asked. His voice sounded hopeful instead of angry.

"We can only try, but I think it will."

"Boy, are you dumb," he said, reverting to his old manners. "Why did it take you a week to think of that? We could have been destroying these things since the minute we got stuck in here."

I didn't defend myself. I could have asked him why *he* hadn't thought of this plan. I could have reminded him that for days he'd spent most of his time complaining. Instead, I saved my energy and set to work.

I climbed up one of the phony trees. I grabbed one of the fake birds that was sitting on a pretend tree limb, and I began to tear it apart. Soon, even with only the little night moons lighting the area, we could see that blue feathers were floating through the air.

Lenox had been chewing on a branch, bending it so he could break it off. But when he saw the feathers raining down, he attacked another bird. This one was a fake cardinal, so the feathers that floated down were a bright red.

After we finished with the birds, I bit off all the flowers so that they lay on the ground. Lenox jumped into the newspaper that the phony human had been holding all these days. He made a huge hole in the middle of it. He jumped on one of the children and knocked him down. I jumped on the other. Then I grabbed a piece of the phony woman's dress in my teeth and pulled

and pulled. Soon the dress was in shreds, and
the woman had almost nothing on, which is
actually the way some humans come to the
park on very hot summer days.

All this activity made us feel good at first.
At last we were doing something that might
help get us out. But after a while, we both

collapsed with exhaustion. Neither of us had ever worked so hard in our lives.

"Listen," I told my cousin as I lay on the ground surrounded by blue and red feathers, bits of newspaper, and broken tree branches. "We don't have to do all of this now. We can do it during the daylight, when people are watching. Let them see how unhappy we are here. Let them realize that this isn't a real world that they're looking at. Squirrels would never harm birds or destroy trees or flowers. Neither you nor I nor any squirrel would ever hurt a human child. The people here at Nu-Tru Styles have turned us into a different type of animal."

So we took the rest of the night off, sleeping to regain our strength. The next day we would continue the devastation in this cage of ours.

CHAPTER TWELVE

The Showdown

There was no way for Lenox and me to be aware of it, but our situation was not unknown in the park. None of the pigeons had reported our plight to our relatives. But one of the photographers who had taken our picture worked for a newspaper. And it was my guinea pig friend PeeWee, with his ability to read, who noticed a page with our picture and a long story about us.

After he read about us, PeeWee spoke to a couple of my siblings who live near his hole. They paid no attention.

"Don't look for trouble, and trouble won't look for you," said one, quoting our mother.

PeeWee refused to give up. He searched Central Park until he found old Uncle Ninety-nine. Now my uncle had never thought much of my friendship with a guinea pig. He believed squirrels should stick with squirrels. He thought nothing good could come of my being pals with the fat, tailless creature who would be competing for the same food as us.

Luckily my uncle had a full stomach and sat still while PeeWee spoke to him. PeeWee had dragged the newspaper all around with him. Of course, my uncle couldn't read the words. But he could look at the photograph.

"It's Lexington and Lenox!" he exclaimed in amazement when he recognized us.

"Yes," PeeWee told him. "That's what I've been saying. They went off on an adventure, and now they are captured in the window of this big store. It says in the newspaper that hundreds of people go out of their way to see the window, which has been called Squirrel World by the store owners."

"Nonsense," said my uncle to PeeWee. "*This* is Squirrel World, not that."

"You're right," said PeeWee. "That's why we have to help rescue them."

"There's nothing we can do," my uncle said. "I'm sorry they were so foolish as to leave the park. But what can we do? Nothing."

"We may not be able to do anything," said PeeWee. "But the humans won't know that. If we gathered hundreds of squirrels in front of the store, I think the humans might realize that Lexington and Lenox should be outside the window, too."

My uncle sat thinking this over. "Do you think we'll find anything good to eat along the way?" he asked. He's a squirrel who is ruled by his stomach more than any other squirrel I've ever met.

"I'm certain of it," said PeeWee, although he told me later this was not true. "I just knew I had to say anything that would get him out of that tree and off to rally the other squirrels."

Anyhow, the lie worked. Uncle Ninety-nine leaped to a nearby tree and summoned several of my cousins, who in turn called to others. Within an hour, there were 400 squirrels ready to set off.

PeeWee wanted to go too, but he realized that his pace was so slow he would never be able to keep up with the squirrels. So instead, he outlined a plan for the squirrels, the way a general would organize a battle. "Wait until dark," he told my family. "If you travel at night, there won't be people around to notice you. Stick close to the sides of buildings. Don't dawdle. Keep moving."

The newspaper article told the exact location of Nu-Tru Styles. And so at dusk that evening, the squirrels set off, knowing exactly where to go.

As I said, I knew none of this at the time. I knew only that when Lenox and I woke with the morning light and looked around at the devastation we had created the night before, there were 367 aunts, uncles, sisters, brothers, and cousins staring at us through the glass and observing that mess, too. (The other 33 relatives had gotten lost or been distracted on their way to Lexington Avenue.)

The sight of our family delighted Lenox and me. It filled us with the energy we needed to return to our task. We immediately began chewing away at the scenery around us. By the time the street began to fill with humans moving in both directions, Lenox and I could see that there was a great deal of unusual activity. There were photographers, sightseers, police cars, and a white truck with those mysterious letters I'd seen on the signs the people carried outside the window:

A-S-P-C-A. I noticed that the truck had a
picture of two dogs and a cat on it, too.

There was such a big crowd that a pretzel
vendor set up business in the middle of the
sidewalk and quickly sold his wares. Some
people threw pieces of their pretzels down
on the ground for our family to eat.

"It's not fair," whined Lenox. "I could use
a pretzel myself."

I ignored him. In fact, I'd gotten pretty good at ignoring his complaints by then. Someday, when Lenox looks to find himself a mate, she will have to be a squirrel who is hard of hearing or can master the art of ignoring his constant moaning and groaning.

In the midst of all this activity, we could hear the lock being opened above us. This meant that the sliding glass door would be opened and a fresh supply of nuts would be thrown into the window. We waited. The door opened, but there were no nuts. Instead, in an instant, we were both pulled off our feet and scooped into a deep net. I tried to keep my balance, but I couldn't. I didn't know what was going to happen next. And just as I feared the worst, the best possible thing happened. The net was turned upside down, and I landed with a thud on the ground outside the window. And Lenox fell beside me.

We heard loud cheers and applause from the people who were standing around.

"Now what?" Lenox cried out above the noise of the crowd.

"Now we are free!" I shouted, because I had quickly realized what had happened.

"Hurray, hurray!" called out those aunts, uncles, brothers, sisters, and cousins whose mouths were not filled with pretzels or an even greater treat that someone had just thrown to them—roasted chestnuts.

PeeWee had not given instructions about returning to the park, but it didn't matter. Our relatives led the march, and the humans seemed to understand that they should keep out of our way. Police officers with loud whistles made the traffic actually come to a stop as we reached Park Avenue. It was amazing that all the cars and buses halted, and not a single life or even a tail was lost under the heavy tires.

By the time we were at Madison Avenue, I could already sniff the scent of the real park—not a phony park with nothing real inside it. It was the honest-to-goodness best place in the world that I could smell. My home in Central Park.

After we crossed Fifth Avenue, I didn't stop to say anything to the other squirrels. Instead, I raced directly to my tree and climbed up into my hole. Nothing had ever felt as wonderful as my nest with its woolen cap for a lining. Within seconds, I was fast asleep. It was dark night when I woke. I saw the moon shining through a cloud, and I lay in my nest, listening to the hushed park sounds: the leaves that moved in the breeze, the flutter of a bird's wing as the bird resettled itself inside a nest. I heard the soft trudge of footsteps crushing dead leaves down below.

I climbed down to the ground. I should not have been surprised, but I was. There was PeeWee, waiting for me.

"Thank goodness you're home again, and all is well," he said.

"I'm happy to be here," I told him. "Lexington Avenue is not all that it's cracked up to be."

"The street should be honored to have your name," he said.

"Thank you," I replied.

"I'm going to bed now," he said. "I'll see you in the morning."

I smiled. How wonderful to know that in the morning I would wake again here at home, among all my friends.

CHAPTER THIRTEEN
Home, Sweet Home

When it was daylight, I again saw PeeWee. This time it was a full reunion, with all his family around him: his mate, Plush, and their offspring, Pudge, Perky, Pip, and Squeak. Plush had grown considerably since I had last seen her, so I wasn't surprised when she announced that in a few weeks there would be another litter of guinea pigs arriving. I'd have a job finding still more holes to house this growing family of theirs. Lenox was right—I did seem to have gone into the real estate business.

PeeWee pulled several newspaper pages from his hole. "You're a very famous squirrel," he told me, "even if they don't know your name."

He read aloud from the newest one, which he had just found that morning:

The window on Lexington Avenue and 59th Street that has caught so much public attention of late is now empty. The two eastern gray squirrels that made it their home for the past ten days seem to have had enough of their artificial environment. They destroyed the plants and other props that they had been living among in an apparent act of protest. Even more amazing was the sight of a thousand squirrels who arrived on the scene to view their mates and lend moral support.

"Stop a minute," I interrupted PeeWee. "There weren't a thousand squirrels on Lexington Avenue, were there?"

"No," said PeeWee, laughing. "It just shows that you can't believe everything you read in the newspaper. But you know, four hundred squirrels in a small area is a lot of squirrels. It probably seemed like a thousand to whoever wrote this article."

"You're right," I agreed. "Go on."

The American Society for the Prevention of Cruelty to Animals had been prepared to liberate the squirrels. "This is the first time in my memory, as acting assistant to the associate director for the New

York City branch, that animals have succeeded to right a grievous wrong," said Carl Goodman. "It proves that squirrels, and indeed all animals, have a social world. I would not be surprised if even the insect populations work together in ways that we have never understood."

People on Lexington Avenue did not analyze the situation. They stood gaping and throwing pieces of their breakfast bagels and doughnuts to the squirrel army. "It was like going to the circus, only better," said Ethan Richardson, age nine. His cousins Juliet and Fiona, who were standing nearby, agreed.

There was a photograph of the window in which Lenox and I had been held captive. I shuddered at the sight. "I will never, ever go to Lexington Avenue again," I vowed.

I was home again and should have been happy, but there was still one problem. I had promised Lenox that I'd accompany him to the street that bore his name. I dreaded the thought, because I had no reason to think it would be a happier journey. But I have always been a squirrel who keeps his promises.

I started out in search of Lenox. He wasn't in Strawberry Fields or the Ramble or any of the other areas of the park. Finally, after hours of running around, I located him in a corner near Turtle Pond. He was sitting on a tree limb, surrounded by half a dozen of our relatives.

"And then I decided that if I tore up all the plants in the window, they'd have to let us go," he said.

For an instant, I felt great anger at my cousin. There he was, bragging about *his* plan and *his* activities. He was making himself out to be a hero when all he'd been was a whining pest during our captivity. But then a breeze came out of nowhere, bringing with it the scent of spring in the park. What did it matter if he wanted to remember our adventure his way? Let him have his admirers, I thought. At least I'm home again.

"Lenox," I called out to him.

He looked down at me, and I saw him shudder. He must have realized that I'd overheard his boasts.

"Hello, Lexi," he said faintly.

"When do you want to leave for Lenox Avenue?" I asked him.

"Are you going to Lenox Avenue, too?" asked one of his listeners.

"Well, to tell you the truth," said Lenox, who a moment before seemed to have forgotten what the word *truth* meant, "I've been thinking. If you've seen one avenue, you've seen them all. So perhaps there's no point to going away again."

"I absolutely agree with you," I said, feeling a wonderful sense of relief.

"You do?" asked Lenox.

"Yes, indeed," I replied. "You and I have had enough adventures to last a lifetime. I'll be perfectly happy to stay right here in the park."

I shook my tail at Lenox and his admirers and turned away. At once, I heard one of the squirrels say to my cousin, "So tell us what happened to you next."

I didn't stay to hear Lenox's version of our expedition. I knew what really happened, and the sooner I could forget about it, the better I would sleep at night. I hurried to my side of the park, looking for PeeWee and his family.

One of the first things I had to do was arrange with PeeWee to give me more reading lessons. I don't expect to go traveling again, but one never knows when the skill of reading will turn out to be useful.

These days, PeeWee's children are foraging farther afield, but PeeWee and Plush are staying closer to home. Soon there will be a new litter of guinea pigs to befriend. Soon the wild strawberries will begin to grow, too. And warm summer nights and humans' picnics, with all their delicious leftovers, are things to look forward to. Oh, life is wonderful!

I feel sorry for all the humans who live in the city and can't spend every minute of their time in the park. But then again, large as the park is, it can't accommodate all the city dwellers all the time. No, Central Park is just the right size for my brothers, sisters, aunts, uncles, cousins, and me. It is just the right size for PeeWee and his family and for the bird population, too. "Come and visit," I whispered to the city at large, "but don't stay too long. This is Squirrel World. It belongs to us."

As I approached my tree, my brother Seventy-four jumped in front of me. "I've heard about your adventures," he told me. "Can I go along with you the next time you go exploring?"

"Sorry," I told him. "You're too late. I'm going to stop right here."